Will Irma Taranee Cornelia Hay Lin

GRAPHIC NOVEL #4

BETWEEN LIGHT AND DARK

W.i.t.c.h.

Will   Irma   Taranee   Cornelia   Hay Lin

GRAPHIC NOVEL #4

BETWEEN LIGHT AND DARK

VOLO

an imprint of
HYPERION BOOKS
FOR CHILDREN
New York

Printed in the United States of America

First Edition
1 3 5 7 9 10 8 6 4 2

ISBN 0-7868-3656-3

Visit www.clubwitch.com

HOW DID I GET SO DIRTY? I HOPE THAT MATT DOESN'T NOTICE.

NO, NOT AT ALL!

AM I LATE?

LUCKILY, YOU'RE EARLY! I HAVE A FAVOR TO ASK YOU.

TODAY MY NEPHEW HAS TO REHEARSE WITH HIS GROUP. . .

WE'RE OFF TO A GOOD START!

. . . AND I MUST TAKE CARE OF A **SPECIAL PATIENT** AT HOME. ARE YOU OKAY STAYING HERE ALONE?

NO PROBLEM!

—IN SPITE OF THE FACT THAT YOU HAVE WARNED ME OF THE CATASTROPHES THAT MIGHT HAPPEN.

HEH! HEH! SEE YOU LATER, THEN.

!!!

YOU HAVE BEEN VERY KIND! GOOD-BYE.

I DON'T BELIEVE IT!

I look forward to embracing my puppy kisses XXX Jackie

IT IS NOT POSSIBLE!!!

PLEASE GIVE IT TO MATT. I TRUST THAT YOU CAN DO THAT, RIGHT?

COME IN, PLEASE. TARANEE WILL BE DOWN IN A MINUTE!

THANKS.

EVEN THOUGH I DON'T KNOW HOW LONG A MINUTE LASTS WHEN TALKING ABOUT MY SISTER.

?!?

HI, NIGEL. I'M ALL SET.

HI.

WELL . . . YOU TWO HAVE FUN.

I GOTTA GO . . . PLENTY OF THINGS TO DO . . . DON'T TRY TO STOP ME . . . BEG ME TO STAY . . .

HAVE YOU PICKED A MOVIE YET?

NO, I THOUGHT I'D LET YOU CHOOSE.

WAIT!

HMMM . . .

I DON'T LIKE THE IDEA OF HER GOING OUT WITH THAT BOY.

DON'T WORRY, MOM! HE'S A GOOD GUY.

STILL . . . MAYBE I SHOULDN'T HAVE LET YOUR SISTER GO OUT WITH HIM.

AFTER ALL . . . LOOK WHAT HAPPENED IN THE MUSEUM.

BY NOW, NIGEL IS OUT OF THE GANG. SO DON'T WORRY.

GOTCHA! THAT'S A POINT FOR ME!

HA-HA!

"I HOPE YOU'RE RIGHT."

YOU KNOW WHAT YOU'RE GONNA GET, RIGHT?

ONLY IF YOU MANAGE TO CATCH ME!

I'M DONE WITH MY HOMEWORK. CAN I GO GO OUT NOW?

AFTER YOU'VE CLEANED UP YOUR ROOM.

SO THAT MEANS I CAN GO OUT SOON.

SNAP

WHAT'S THAT?

MY DIARY FROM LAST YEAR. FULL OF ALL MY THOUGHTS AND MEMORIES.

DIARY

I THOUGHT I HAD LOST IT.

FRUSHH

You are nice
You are lively
You are the friend I like
You are nice
You are okay
Stay the same
Elyon

"ELYON!"

"THINGS WERE SO DIFFERENT THEN."

CLAP CLAP

THIRD PLACE! YOU WERE GREAT!

I STILL CAN'T BELIEVE IT!

NEXT TIME BET YOU'LL IN THE GOLD!

YOU'RE MY LUCKY CHARM, ELLIE!

SERIOUSLY . . . DID YOU REALLY TURN DOWN PETE'S INVITATION?

I DID.

I'M JUST GLAD YOU KEEP COMING TO WATCH.

AND YOU KNOW WHY.

BECAUSE OF THE BOY IN YOUR DREAMS?

HOW COULD IT HAPPEN?

"WHY HAVE WE BECOME ENEMIES?"

ALL OF HEATHERFIELD IS COVERED BY A WHITE BLANKET OF SNOW.

YUCK! I LOOK LIKE AN **ENDANGERED SPECIES** IN THIS OUTFIT.

I SHOULD TRY AGAIN. I HAVE TO FIND SOMETHING THAT WILL LEAVE MATT BREATHLESS.

EXCUSE ME, I'M LOOKING FOR WILL. SHE'S A FRIEND OF MINE. HAVE YOU SEEN HER?

QUIT JOKING AROUND. THIS IS SERIOUS BUSINESS!

WHAT DO YOU THINK?

DO YOU REALLY WANT MY **HONEST** OPINION?

NO. I THINK MINE IS ENOUGH!

IF YOU'RE USING YOUR POWERS TO CHANGE YOUR LOOK, THERE MUST BE SOMETHING WRONG. WHAT'S GOING ON?

MMM . . . DON'T MAKE ME THINK ABOUT IT.

IF YOU SAY SO. HOWEVER, I NEED TO TALK TO YOU ABOUT ELYON.

WHAT ABOUT HER?

BEFORE WE BECAME GUARDIANS OF THE VEIL, SHE WAS DIFFERENT!

SHE HAS BEEN MY FRIEND FOR YEARS! I DON'T UNDERSTAND WHO SHE HAS BECOME.

I WANT TO KNOW WHY SHE HAS CHANGED AND IF THERE IS ANYTHING LEFT OF THE GIRL I KNEW.

BUT THE ONLY WAY I CAN FIND OUT IS BY GOING TO MERIDIAN AND TALKING TO HER FACE TO FACE.

...

THAT'S A CRAZY IDEA, AND YOU KNOW IT!

"WILL HAS ONLY SEEN ELYON'S WORST SIDE. SHE CAN'T UNDERSTAND."

"IRMA AND HAY LIN KNEW HER. THEY'LL KNOW WHY I HAVE TO DO THIS."

GREAT IDEA, CORNY! IF YOU WANT TO UNLEASH CEDRIC AND ALL HIS MUSCLE MEN AGAINST YOU, THAT IS THE PERFECT PLAN.

IRMA'S RIGHT. IT SOUNDS DANGEROUS.

OH, NEVER MIND!

16

I UNDERSTAND IF YOU DON'T AGREE.

I WOULDN'T WANT TO END UP IN THE **MERIDIAN** PRISON. WOULD YOU?

CORNELIA! STOP! WAIT!

HAY LIN!

PLEASE EXAMINE THOSE STALACTITES! AND WATCH THE SOLIDIFICATION PROCESS OF THE WATER AND BE SURE TO TAKE A PICTURE OF IT.

URGH! YES, MA'AM.

SKREEEK

SHE CAN'T GET TO MERIDIAN WITH THE HEART OF CANDRACAR, CAN SHE?

I DON'T THINK SO!

"I GUESS I HAVE TO DO THIS ON MY OWN."

WHO'S THERE?

WHOEVER YOU ARE, COME OUT!

COME ON! I KNOW YOU'RE IN THERE!

?

YOU?!

I DIDN'T THINK I'D FIND YOU HERE!

GET READY TO FIGHT THE POWERS OF EARTH!

I WON'T FIGHT YOU!

NO? WHY NOT?

VATHEK!

I'VE SEEN WHAT **CEDRIC** HAS DONE.

WHAT ARE YOU TALKING ABOUT?

DO YOU MEAN YOU'VE TURNED AGAINST HIM?

I'VE ONLY OPENED MY EYES.

MY PEOPLE HAVE BEEN SUFFERING FOR TOO LONG BECAUSE OF **PHOBOS**. NOW I WILL HELP THOSE WHO FIGHT TO BRING JOY AND PEACE TO MERIDIAN ONCE AGAIN!

I'M DONE! I HAVE EVERYTHING CALEB ASKED FOR.

CALEB . . .

CALEB

CALEB

CALEB

WHAT'S HAPPENING??? THAT NAME . . .

IT'S NOT POSSIBLE!

CLANG

GOOD-BYE, GUARDIAN!

WAIT! TAKE ME WITH YOU!

IF YOU HAVE CHANGED, MAYBE ELYON HAS, TOO . . .

MMM . . . DON'T COUNT ON IT. SHE IS A SLAVE TO CEDRIC!

BUT WE CAN TRY, ANYWAY. WHO KNOWS.

A LOT OF COURAGE IS NEEDED

TO FACE THE PROBLEMS

20

TO OFFER A FLOWER

AND TO MAKE A CHOICE.

BUT JUST HOW MUCH COURAGE IS NEEDED . . .

. . . IN MERIDIAN?

I DON'T UNDERSTAND ANYMORE. YOU HAVE TO EXPLAIN EVERYTHING, CEDRIC!

TRY TO BE QUIET!

NO! YOU ATTACKED WILL AFTER SHE SAVED YOUR LIFE!

IT'S SHAMEFUL BEHAVIOR FOR ANYBODY!

HA-HA-HA! GROW UP, LITTLE GIRL!

YOU CANNOT THINK LIKE A STUDENT ANYMORE. YOU ARE A **PRINCESS** NOW!

YOU ARE RIGHT!

SO I ORDER YOU TO LEAVE ME ALONE!

WHERE ARE YOU GOING?

I WANT TO SEE MERIDIAN. **ALONE!**

I WANT TO UNDERSTAND WHY PEOPLE TRY TO LEAVE THIS PLACE!

"AND TO FIND THE CAUSE OF THE PAIN THAT IS PRESENT HERE IN METAWORLD!"

WHY DID THE GUARD BURN OUR HOUSES?

DON'T ASK ANY QUESTIONS, LITTLE ONE.

MUMMY SAYS IT'S PHO—

DON'T SAY ANOTHER WORD.

PHOBOS? MY BROTHER?

YOU'RE SAFE NOW!

I CAN'T BELIEVE IT.

HE CAN'T REALLY EXIST!

SHE IS NOT ONE OF US!

SHE CANNOT STAY HERE!

SHE IS HORRIBLE TO LOOK AT!

EXCUSE ME! HAVE YOU EVER LOOKED IN A MIRROR?

25

BE QUIET! I CAN VOUCH FOR HER!

WHAT A PERFECT THING TO SAY.

SHE'LL BRING US PROBLEMS!

CALEB! THEY'RE COMING!

THE SOLDIERS SPOTTED US! THEY ARE ABOUT TO ATTACK.

IT'S HOPELESS.

I KNEW IT!

IT'S THE END!

STOP IT!

I TOLD YOU THAT YOU'D CAUSE PROB-LEMS.

VATHEK! TAKE THE GROUP WITH YOU! THE OTHERS WILL FOLLOW ME.

ALL RIGHT.

COME ON, LET'S GO!

THEY'RE CLOSE. I CAN FEEL IT.

WE'LL NEVER MAKE IT!

QUICK! THEY MUST NOT CATCH US!

LEAVE ME ALONE!

THAT VOICE . . .

SBRA AANG

STOP THEM!

WHAT DO WE DO?

LET'S JOIN FORCES!

POWERS OF THE EARTH!

ZOOOT

WELL . . . I DON'T KNOW WHAT POWER THIS IS, BUT I HOPE IT WORKS!

RUN!

MOVE! HELP!

29

RUUUMBLE

WHAT DID WE DO?

OOPS . . . MAYBE THAT WAS A LITTLE TOO MUCH.

WHAT HAVE WE DONE?

WE HAVE CAUSED . . .

". . . AN EARTHQUAKE IN MERIDIAN!"

BROOOMM

AND IN HEATHERFIELD . . .

BBROAMM

YIKES . . . EVERYONE, BE CALM! IT'S ONLY A LITTLE RUMBLE.

A LITTLE?

I THINK MRS. VARGAS IS JUST TRYING TO REASSURE US.

WHAT'S HAPPENING?

CANDRACAR

THEY SHOULDN'T HAVE DONE THAT! THEY HAVE UNLEASHED DARK FORCES!

BY TEAMING UP, CORNELIA AND ELYON HAVE OPENED A PASSAGE IN THE VEIL.

EARTH AND MERIDIAN ARE IN DANGER!

THE GUARDIANS ARE NOT DOING THEIR DUTY!

HUSH! LET DESTINY TAKE ITS COURSE . . .

B-RING

. . . LET THE GIRLS FIND THEMSELVES, AND YOU MUST FIND YOUR TRUST IN THEM.

WE WERE
ALL SO
SCARED!

SCARED?
WHY?

IT WAS ONLY
A LITTLE
EARTHQUAKE.
THERE WERE
NO MONSTERS
INVOLVED.

HEE-HEE-
HEE!

!!!

COMPARED
TO OUR MORE
RECENT
ADVENTURES,
THIS IS
NOTHING.

L—
L—
LOOK . . .

L—L—
LOOK . . .

WOW!
LOOKS LIKE
WE HAVE
MORE DAMAGE
THAN WE
THOUGHT.

TRUE!
BUT IT HAS
NOTHING TO DO
WITH ME:
LOOK!

AAGH!

TELL US THE TRUTH. YOU WERE HELD HOSTAGE BY A GROUP OF FIERCE AND TOTALLY BACKWARD STYLISTS, RIGHT?

HMMM . . . I SMELL A DATE!

JUST LIKE TARANEE DID WITH NIGEL. WILL HASN'T TOLD US ABOUT THE BIG DATE YET!

I NEVER SAID I WENT OUT WITH NIGEL!

YOU FORGET— I HAVE POWERS!

SO? WHAT'S UP, WILL?

NOTHING!

I JUST WANTED TO CHANGE MY LOOK!

GIVE IT TO MATT, PLEASE!

WELL, TO TELL YOU THE TRUTH, YOU HAVE CHANGED!

YOU DON'T LOOK LIKE WILL!

THAT'S ALREADY SOMETHING!

LET'S TALK ABOUT SOMETHING ELSE, OKAY? WHY WAS THIS MEETING SO IMPORTANT, HAY LIN?

I ALMOST FORGOT!

SPLAT

33

LUCKILY, I HAVE MY HANDS!

AND NOW YOUR FOREHEAD, TOO!

9AM

MAP

OKAY, WHAT IS IT?

SHOULDN'T WE WAIT FOR CORNELIA?

I CALLED HER A BUNCH OF TIMES, BUT SHE WASN'T HOME.

PLEASE TELL ME SHE HAS NOTHING TO DO WITH THIS . . .

RIGHT?

WHAT ARE YOU TALKING ABOUT? WHY WOULD THE EARTHQUAKE INVOLVE CORNELIA?

CORNELIA WANTED TO GO TO MERIDIAN TO FIND ELYON.

"BUT SHE COULDN'T HAVE DONE IT ALONE, RIGHT?"

FSSHHH

?

LOOKS LIKE THE SOLDIERS ARE GONE.

I WAS IN THE MIDDLE OF THE WORST MOMENT OF MY LIFE AND YOU APPEARED!

AS IF NOTHING HAD CHANGED BETWEEN US.

I'M HERE FOR THAT VERY REASON.

OUR DESTINY CAN'T BE TO FIGHT EACH OTHER.

WE WERE FRIENDS!

BEST FRIENDS.

DON'T SAY WE *WERE*. WE CAN BE FRIENDS AGAIN!

I'D LIKE THAT, BUT DO YOU THINK IT IS STILL POSSIBLE?

I KNOW I'VE MADE MISTAKES. I'VE DONE HORRIBLE THINGS TO ALL OF YOU.

CEDRIC CHANGED MY LIFE. HE FILLED MY HEAD WITH LIES . . .

AND I BELIEVED HIM!

AND NOW?

I DON'T KNOW. I DON'T EVEN KNOW WHO I AM ANYMORE!

IN HEATHERFIELD, I HAVE NOTHING.

AND HERE I'M THE PRINCESS OF A WORLD THAT DOESN'T WANT ME.

WE'LL FIX EVERYTHING. I DON'T KNOW HOW, BUT WE'LL DEFINITELY FIX IT . . . TOGETHER.

MERIDIAN DOES NOT LOOK FOR ANYTHING BUT YOUR LIGHT, YOUR MAJESTY.

WHAT?

AND THE REBELLION IS READY TO SERVE YOU!

UNDERGROUND, IN THE SUBWAY SYSTEMS OF HEATHERFIELD
PLIC PLIC
LOOK! HERE'S A PASSAGE!
THIS PLACE IS JUST ABSOLUTELY BEAUTIFUL! I REALLY WISH I LIVED HERE.
I'VE NEVER SEEN A PORTAL OPEN AT THE AMUSEMENT PARK.
YEAH, WELL, MAYBE THIS ONE WILL LEAD RIGHT TO THE PALACE.
WELL . . . THAT WOULD BE CONVENIENT.
WHAT IS THIS PLACE?
THIS IS DEFINITELY NOT A BUILDING IN HEATHERFIELD.
MAYBE IT IS SOME KIND OF GIFT FROM METAMOOR?
LOOK!

IF THIS IS NOT THE WORK OF CORNELIA . . .

SHE IS IN MERIDIAN. I DON'T KNOW HOW SHE DID IT, BUT SHE'S HERE.

NOW THE ONLY THING MISSING IS A NICE LITTLE MONSTER THAT IS TRYING TO KILL US . . . THAT WOULD MAKE ME FEEL AT HOME.

PLEASE DON'T SAY THAT! THIS PLACE FREAKS ME OUT.

DON'T WORRY. I WAS ONLY JOKING AROUND.

MAYBE YOU'RE SCARED BECAUSE THOSE FACES ARE STARING RIGHT AT US.

WHO DO YOU THINK THEY ARE?

THEY SEEM TO BE GENTLEWOMEN.

MAYBE THEY LIVED IN THIS PALACE!

THIS PORTRAIT IS THE MOST STRIKING OF ALL.

DOESN'T SHE LOOK FAMILIAR?

BUT WHAT . . .

FSHHH

IN FRONT OF THE PORTAL, DREAMS AND FEARS OVERLAP ONE ANOTHER.

THIS IS OUR LAST CHANCE. MAYBE, BY GOING THROUGH THE PORTAL, WE'LL REACH A BETTER PLACE.

I DON'T WANT TO GO!

IF THE PEOPLE GO THROUGH THE OPENING ALL AT THE SAME TIME, IT WILL BE HORRIFIC.

I AM THE CAUSE OF THIS DISASTER.

I HAVE TO GO BACK TO HEATHERFIELD AND CLOSE THE PORTAL.

AT LEAST YOU CAN DO SOMETHING, CORNELIA.

BELIEVE ME, YOUR MAJESTY...

" . . . YOU CAN DO A LOT FOR THIS WORLD!"

ARE WE SURE THIS IS THE RIGHT CHOICE?

I DON'T UNDERSTAND. YOU BELONG TO THE REBEL FORCES THAT FIGHT AGAINST MY BROTHER.

WHY DO YOU WANT TO HELP ME, IF YOU KNOW WHO I AM?

WHAT I'M WONDERING IS . . .

DO YOU KNOW WHO YOU REALLY ARE?

THE LEGITIMATE HEIR TO THE THRONE OF MERIDIAN HAS COME BACK!

?!

HERE IS PRINCESS ELYON!

"THERE IS STILL HOPE FOR MERIDIAN!"

WE'RE ON YOUR SIDE!

I HELD YOU IN MY ARMS WHEN YOU WERE JUST A BABY!

YEEE YU HOO!

YOU'LL PUNISH PHOBOS BECAUSE HE HAS BEEN BAD, RIGHT, PRINCESS?

WELCOME TO MERIDIAN.

WHAT DO I DO?

"...DON'T GO AWAY!"

YOU WON'T LEAVE US, WILL YOU?

WE BEG YOU!

I PROMISE. BUT DON'T BEG ANYMORE, PLEASE.

GIVE US THE **REBELS!**

THOSE WHO SIDE WITH THE REBELS WILL SUFFER THE CONSEQUENCES.

I WOULD BE HAPPY TO SHOW YOU WHAT HE MEANS.

45

GO AWAY!

BOW DOWN TO YOUR QUEEN!

GET THEM!

YOU CAN'T DO THIS ALONE!

GO AND FIND SHELTER!

RUN FOR YOUR LIVES!

WOW! THAT WAS AN UNCOMFORTABLE TRIP!

I'M JUST GLAD WE MADE IT.

ZOING

GASP! I TAKE IT BACK!

STUMP

WE HAVE TO SAVE THE PRINCESS.

???

WANT SOME HELP?

WOOSH

WHOA! UNEXPECTED BUT TOTALLY APPRECIATED!

SHAATZ

WOOSH

AN ATTACK TODAY, THE ENEMY IS BLOWN AWAY!

WOOSH

YOUR ATTACK ISN'T NEARLY AS BAD AS YOUR RHYME, IRMA!

47

WHEN YOU GET A MINUTE, MAYBE YOU CAN TELL US WHAT IS GOING ON.

YOU GUYS ARE NEVER GOING TO BELIEVE ME.

FWZZ

"BUT I WASN'T WRONG ABOUT ELYON!"

PLONG

WATCH OUT!

HEY!

TUMP

STAY CALM!

TUMP

BE CAREFUL, DON'T HURT YOURSELF!

"YOU HAVE FAILED . . . AGAIN."

"YOU KNOW YOUR DESTINY, LORD CEDRIC."

AAARGH!

I CONDEMN YOU TO . . .

AAAGH . . . WAIT, PLEASE . . .

GIVE THE PEOPLE WHAT THEY ARE ASKING FOR!

IT WILL MAKE YOUR SISTER FEEL STRONGER, AND THEN SHE WILL BE READY TO BE ABSORBED SOONER.

FINE, THEN MAKE IT SO.

"AND DON'T FAIL ME AGAIN. BECAUSE THE NEXT FAILURE WILL BE YOUR LAST."

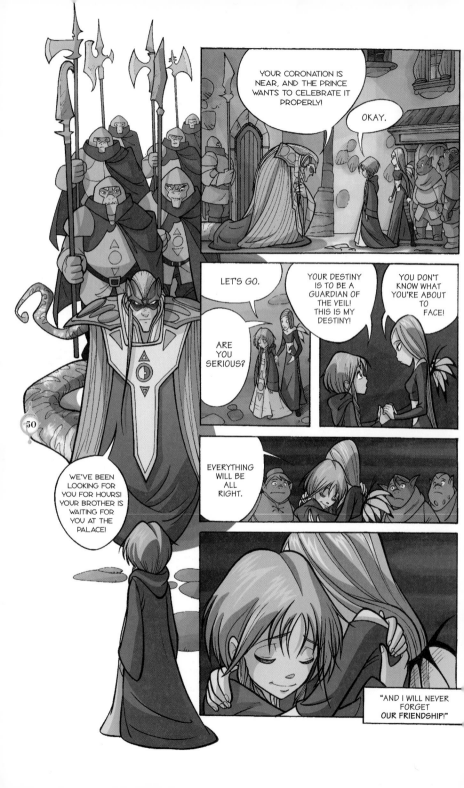

I GUESS WE CAN GO BACK TO HEATHERFIELD.

I WISH WE DIDN'T HAVE TO MAKE ANOTHER TRIP THROUGH THAT DISGUSTING MUSH!

IF YOU KNOW A MORE COMFORTABLE WAY, I'D BE HAPPY TO HEAR IT!

WHERE ARE YOU GOING?

I'LL BE RIGHT BACK.

I'LL NEVER SEE HIM AGAIN!

I HAVE TO TELL HIM!

51

UM . . . I JUST WANTED . . .

WELL . . . I WANTED TO TELL YOU THAT . . . I'VE SEEN YOU BEFORE.

I KNOW.

"YOU DON'T NEED TO EXPLAIN."

IT WAS WRITTEN THAT ELYON WOULD COME BACK, AS IT WAS WRITTEN THAT WE WOULD MEET AGAIN.

I BELIEVE THAT.

"I'VE BEEN DREAMING OF YOU EVER SINCE."

AND IF WE'VE LOVED EACH OTHER IN OUR DREAMS, THE VEIL WILL NOT BE ABLE TO DIVIDE US!

I CAN'T BELIEVE THIS IS REALLY HAPPENING!

DO YOU KNOW WHAT THIS IS?

A TEAR?

LOOK CLOSELY!

"IT'S A PROMISE."

AND HERE I WAS THINKING CORNELIA WAS COLD AND RATIONAL!

BUT SHE IS THE EXACT OPPOSITE. AH, LOOOOOVE!

SOMEONE IS GLAD SHE CAME TO MERIDIAN TO LOOK FOR ELYON!

53

UM . . . NOW WE CAN GO.

I DON'T THINK WE CAN GO WITHOUT SOME INFORMATION!

I THINK YOU SHOULD TELL US MORE ABOUT WHAT WE JUST SAW!

COME IN, PRINCESS! YOUR BROTHER IS WAITING FOR YOU!

MY BELOVED SISTER!

PHOBOS...

I'VE BEEN LOOKING FORWARD TO THIS MOMENT FOR A LONG TIME.

IT'S A PITY WE HAD TO LEAVE THAT PALACE IN METAMOOR! IT WASN'T SO BAD.

DID YOU WANT TO RENT IT FOR THE NEXT SCHOOL PARTY?

I'M GOING TO RUN INSIDE.

SEE YOU TOMORROW!

HEY! IT'S NOT WORTH THE EFFORT!

SHE CAN'T ESCAPE FROM US FOREVER!

SOONER OR LATER, SHE'LL HAVE TO TELL US EVERYTHING!

GOOD EVENING, EVERYONE!

YOU'RE LATE. I HAVEN'T EATEN YET, AND I'M HUNGRY.

DINNER WILL BE READY IN FIVE MINUTES!

UGH! SHE ALWAYS TREATS ME LIKE A LITTLE BOY!

WHEN SHE BROUGHT HOME THE **PUPPY**, SHE EVEN TOLD ME THAT I LOOK LIKE HER BABY BROTHER!

UM . . . WHICH PUPPY?

HER SAINT BERNARD PUPPY! MY GRANDFATHER CAN'T TAKE CARE OF IT IN THE SHOP, BECAUSE IT'S TOO BIG.

OH! I UNDERSTAND.

HE ISN'T THE PUPPY SHE WANTS TO EMBRACE!

CONTROL YOURSELF, OR HE'LL FIND OUT!

WELL . . . NEVER LOSE YOUR HEAD OVER SOMEONE OLDER THAN YOU!

YES! I KNOW!

MAY I WALK YOU HOME?

" IT WOULD BE A PLEASURE. . . . "

HEATHERFIELD

DESPITE THE COLD AND SNOW THAT COVER THE AREA NOW, IN JUST A FEW DAYS, THIS WILL BE ONE OF THE HOTTEST SPOTS IN THE CITY.

63

AND THE REASON BEHIND THIS SUDDEN RISE IN TEMPERATURE? KARMILLA AND HER BAND—AND UNLESS YOU ARE FROM ANOTHER PLANET . . .

SUNDAY from 4 P.M. till night

POP & ROCK

KARMILLA

. . . YOU'VE HEARD OF HER!

I SAID NO! PLEASE DON'T MAKE ME. . . .

YOUR TABLE SEEMS TO BE MAKING A LOT OF NOISE, YOUNG LADIES! WHY DON'T YOU TRY KEEPING YOUR MOUTHS CLOSED WHILE YOU WORK?

YOUR WATERCOLOR IS STUNNING, HAY LIN! YOU HAVE A GOOD BRUSH TECHNIQUE AND A GOOD EYE FOR COLOR.

SURE! GOT IT! NO PROBLEM!

AND THE LIKENESS IS EXCELLENT! YOU'RE REALLY QUITE TALENTED!

THANK YOU, MRS. WHARTON!

HERE, ON THE OTHER HAND, I CAN'T REALLY SAY THE SAME THING! WHY DON'T YOU TRY APPLYING YOURSELF A LITTLE MORE, IRMA?

DUH-OH . . .

OOOF! THIS IS RIDICULOUS. I HATE PAINTING! IS IT MY FAULT IF I'M NOT AS AMAZING AS SOME PEOPLE?

YOU COULD PROBABLY DO SOMETHING ABOUT IT . . .

AFTER ALL, WE'RE WORKING WITH WATERCOLORS. AND SINCE YOU DO CONTROL THE POWER OF WATER . . . IT SHOULDN'T BE TOO DIFFICULT FOR YOU!

GOOD POINT, TARANEE!

I THINK THAT IS CALLED CHEATING!

OH, LIGHTEN UP! THERE'S NOTHING WRONG WITH WANTING A GOOD GRADE IN DRAWING. JUST THINK HOW IMPRESSED MRS. WHARTON WILL BE!

HERE WE GO . . . IT'S WORKING . . . IT'S REALLY WORKING!

DRIIIIIN

SCHOOL IS OVER FOR THE DAY.

SO WHAT ARE YOU UP TO THIS AFTERNOON?

BESIDES STUDYING? NOT MUCH! I MIGHT GO WITH MY MOM TO LOOK FOR A NEW PAIR OF SKATES! I'M A LITTLE BEHIND WITH MY TRAINING, AND IT WOULD BE A GOOD EXCUSE TO START AGAIN.

WHAT ABOUT YOU?

STUDYING, STUDYING, AND MORE STUDYING.

HI, MOM!

I'M GLAD YOU'RE HOME! COULD YOU GIVE ME A HAND WITH THESE SHOPPING BAGS? THEY WEIGH A TON!

HUFF... WHAT'S WITH ALL THESE GROCERIES?

THEY'RE FOR THIS SUNDAY! I WANT THE PARTY TO BE PERFECT!

THE... PARTY?

DON'T TELL ME YOU FORGOT? IT'S MY BIRTHDAY!

OF COURSE I DIDN'T FORGET! IT'S... IT'S JUST THAT I DIDN'T THINK YOU WERE HAVING A PARTY...

IT'S A PRIVATE LUNCH PARTY, ACTUALLY, JUST FOR THE TWO OF US! ISN'T THAT GREAT?

AND THEN, AFTERWARDS, WE'LL TAKE A TRIP TO ROSEVILLE! IT'S BEEN SO LONG SINCE WE DID ANYTHING FUN LIKE THAT!

IT'S A FANTASTIC IDEA, MOM! THERE'S JUST ONE LITTLE PROBLEM...

I CAN'T DO IT THIS SUNDAY! THERE'S A CONCERT IN TOWN, AND THE GIRLS AND I ARE GOING! IRMA'S DAD IS TAKING US . . .

I HAD REALLY HOPED TO SPEND THE DAY WITH YOU.

WE CAN ALWAYS GO TO ROSEVILLE NEXT WEEKEND . . .

NEXT WEEKEND IT WON'T BE MY BIRTHDAY ANYMORE! I'M SORRY, WILL . . .

. . . BUT WE NEVER SEE EACH OTHER ANYMORE. YOU SPEND ALL YOUR TIME ALONE OR WITH YOUR FRIENDS!

WHAT AM I SUPPOSED TO DO? IT'S NOT MY FAULT YOU'RE NEVER HERE!

I HAVE TO WORK, WILL! YOU ALWAYS SEEM TO FORGET THAT!

I KNOW! BUT YOU ALWAYS MANAGE TO FIND TIME FOR MR. COLLINS, DON'T YOU?

DON'T USE THAT TONE OF VOICE WITH ME! KEEP IT UP AND THIS SUNDAY'S PLANS ARE GOING TO LOOK A LOT DIFFERENT . . .

. . . YOU WON'T BE GOING TO THE CONCERT, AND I WON'T BE GIVING ANY BIRTHDAY PARTY! WE'LL BOTH STAY AT HOME LIKE TWO FOOLS. NOW, THIS CONVERSATION IS OVER!

BACK IN HEATHERFIELD, SUNDAY HAS FINALLY ARRIVED. CERTAIN PEOPLE HAVE BEEN WAITING ALL WEEK FOR THIS DAY . . .

. . . BUT GREAT EXPECTATIONS CAN SOMETIMES BRING GREAT DISAPPOINTMENTS, TOO!

BELIEVE ME, IRMA! I'M SORRIER THAN YOU! IT'S JUST A MILD CASE OF THE FLU, BUT I'D RATHER BE SAFE THAN SORRY! I'LL BE THERE FOR THE NEXT CONCERT, OKAY?

FIRST **WILL**, AND NOW YOU! WHAT'S UP WITH YOU GUYS? THIS WAS GOING TO BE THE BEST DAY EVER! WHO KNOWS WHEN WE'LL GET ANOTHER CHANCE LIKE THIS?

LET'S GO, IRMA! WE'RE GOING TO BE LATE!

WELL, YOUR LOSS, HAY LIN. AND EVEN THOUGH YOU DON'T DESERVE IT, I'LL PICK YOU UP SOME AUTOGRAPHS. HOPE YOU FEEL BETTER!

I DON'T LIKE LYING TO MY FRIENDS . . . BUT IF I TOLD THEM THE TRUTH THEY WOULD HAVE MADE FUN OF ME FOREVER!

SKIPPING OUT ON A CONCERT TO HELP YOUR PARENTS OUT AT THE RESTAURANT IS NOT THE COOLEST THING TO DO . . .

WHAT . . . NO CANDLES?

NO CANDLES. HERE'S YOUR SLICE . . .

IF YOU DON'T WANT IT NOW, YOU CAN HAVE IT LATER!

I WON'T WANT IT LATER, EITHER. I'M NOT HUNGRY.

WILL . . .

E HERE, MOUSE! 'S GO OR A K . . .

SAY SOMETHING, SUSAN! DON'T LET HER GO OFF ANGRY! STOP HER!

THAT WAS GREAT, SUSAN. REAL GREAT.

SLAM

IT'S A SAD SUNDAY . . .

. . . WHEN I'M LOOKING FORWARD TO MONDAY! THAT'S PROBABLY THE FIRST TIME THAT'S HAPPENED TO ME SINCE WE MOVED TO HEATHERFIELD!

I HOPE HAY LIN IS ENJOYING HERSELF! AT LEAST SHE **DECIDED** NOT TO GO TO THE CONCERT . . . **SOMEBODY ELSE** MADE MY DECISION FOR ME!

HAY LIN! PHONE CALL FOR YOU!

I'LL TAKE IT UPSTAIRS!

DO YOU THINK YOU CAN HANDLE THIS ALL BY YOURSELF? IT'S EASY! JUST WRITE DOWN THE ORDER AND GIVE IT TO THE COOK! I'LL BE RIGHT BACK!

WILL! HOW ARE YOU? DID YOU AND YOUR MOM MAKE UP? HUH?

WHAT DO YOU MEAN?

I'M TALKING ABOUT THE FACT THAT WE ARE STILL FIGHTING! IT'S DIFFICULT TO EXPLAIN! NOTHING IS WRONG, SPECIFICALLY... I JUST DON'T WANT TO MAKE UP WITH HER QUITE YET...

...PLEASE, HAY LIN! DON'T YOU YELL AT ME, TOO! YOU'RE MY FRIEND—YOU SHOULD BE CHEERING ME UP!

OKAY, OKAY! I'LL TELL YOU SOMETHING FUNNY. THEN! LISTEN...

UH-OH...

WILL! THE MAP OF THE TWELVE PORTALS IS FLASHING!

THAT'S NOT EVEN FUNNY, HAY LIN...

I'M NOT JOKING! IT'S AN EMERGENCY!

"A PORTAL OPENED UP SOMEWHERE INSIDE THE STADIUM!"

SO, I GUESS I'M GOING TO THE STADIUM AFTER ALL, SINCE MOM'S NOT GOING TO BE HAPPY IF SHE FINDS OUT. I'LL HAVE TO GET HOME BEFORE SHE REALIZES . . .

HOPEFULLY HAY LIN WILL BE ABLE TO COME AND HELP ME, SINCE I HAVE NO CLUE WHERE THE OTHER GIRLS ARE. I GUESS FOR NOW, I'VE GOT TO DO THIS BY MYSELF!

FIRST, I HAVE TO FIGURE OUT A WAY INSIDE—WITHOUT A TICKET, I DOUBT THESE TWO GOONS WILL LET ME JUST WALTZ RIGHT IN . . .

. . . BUT MAYBE THE HEART OF CANDRACAR CAN HELP! CLOSE YOUR EYES, DORMOUSE!

DON'T MAKE THAT FACE, DORMOUSE! IT'S STILL ME.

EERK!

THEY HAVE HIDDEN THEMSELVES WELL. BUT I CAN STILL FEEL THEM!

OH, NO! WHAT AM I GOING TO DO?

DORMOUSE!

WHERE DID THAT COME FROM?

STOP THAT CREATURE!

AAAAUGH!

YIK

GNIK!

COWARDS! ARE YOU REALLY AFRAID OF THIS PATHETIC CREATURE?

B—BUT IT WAS SO . . . HAIRY! HAVE YOU EVER SEEN ANYTHING SO HORRIBLE?

OH, NO! MY DORMOUSE ENTERED THE PORTAL! COME BACK . . . PLEASE . . .

. . . COME BACK!

WOW! WHO KNEW MY DORMOUSE COULD RUN SO FAST? MAYBE IF I CALL, IT'LL STOP...

...BUT HOW WOULD I DO THAT? I'VE HAD THE LITTLE GUY FOR SO LONG AND I STILL HAVEN'T GIVEN IT A NAME! WHEN, AND IF, I GET HOME, THE FIRST THING I'M GOING TO DO IS FIX THAT PROBLEM!

GNIK!

OKAY, THIS IS ENOUGH! STOP!

?

!

ARE YOU SPEAKING TO ME? IF YOU WANTED TO BE FUNNY, YOU PICKED THE WRONG PERSON TO PLAY WITH!

OOPS...

YOU LITTLE BEAST! IT SEEMS THAT GETTING INTO TROUBLE IS YOUR SPECIALITY...

DO YOU THINK YOU COULD FINISH DRYING THE PLATES, DAD? I HAVE TO MAKE AN IMPORTANT PHONE CALL!

CERTAINLY, MY DEAR, BUT . . .

THANKS, DAD! I'LL BE BACK DOWN SOON!

I WONDER IF WILL MANAGED TO GET INTO THE STADIUM WITHOUT ANY TROUBLE?

I REALLY HOPE SHE'S OKAY!

BRIIIP BRIIIP

COME ON, WILL . . . PICK UP!

94

THE PERSON YOU ARE CALLING IS CURRENTLY UNAVAILABLE. PLEASE TRY AGAIN LATER. THIS IS A RECORDING.

UNAVAILABLE?

WHERE ARE YOU, WILL?

WHERE AM I? HOW DID I GET HERE?

OH, DORMOUSE! YOU DIDN'T LEAVE ME ALONE AFTER ALL!

UH-OH . . .

PLEASE, DON'T BE AFRAID OF ME. MY NAME IS DALTAR. I AM NOT HERE TO HARM YOU.

I'D TELL YOU WHY, BUT IT'S A LONG STORY...

I'M LISTENING.

LISTEN TO ME, PRINCESS ELYON! YOU COULD DO A LOT FOR THIS WORLD.

FIGHT BESIDE US FOR THE FREEDOM OF MERIDIAN!

THE FREEDOM OF MERIDIAN...

I SOMETIMES FEEL LIKE I'M THE ONLY ONE WHO DOESN'T KNOW THE TRUTH.

CALEB TELLS ME ONE THING...

CEDRIC ANOTHER...

WHOM DO I BELIEVE?

ONCE UPON A TIME, THESE PEOPLE WERE MY MOTHER AND FATHER . . . IN SOME WAYS, THEY STILL ARE!

I GREW UP WITH THEM! I LOVED THEM . . . BUT SOMETHING CHANGED . . .

" . . . BACK IN HEATHERFIELD . . ."

THEY ARE REBELS, ELYON! TWO HORRIBLE CREATURES WHO TOOK YOU AWAY FROM YOUR REAL HOME AND YOUR REAL FAMILY!

THAT'S HARD TO BELIEVE, CEDRIC!

YOU WILL GET USED TO YOUR NEW LIFE, I PROMISE! NOW, LET'S GO.

PACK UP YOUR THINGS AND GET READY TO LEAVE!

?!

ELYON! WHAT'S GOING ON?

DAD! MOM!

DON'T CALL THEM THAT, ELYON . . .

PHOBOS IS EVIL, ELYON! THAT IS ALL YOU NEED TO KNOW . . . HE HAS TAKEN OVER AND CONTROLLED YOUR REIGN FOR ALL THESE YEARS!

WE TOOK YOU AWAY TO RESCUE YOU— NOT TO HURT YOU! YOUR BROTHER IS THE CRUEL ONE . . .

WE WANTED YOU TO GROW UP HAPPY, FAR AWAY FROM A WORLD WITH NO HOPE! PLEASE FORGIVE US! WE DID IT ALL FOR YOU!

PHOBOS MAY HAVE MADE SOME MISTAKES IN THE PAST, BUT HE'S CHANGED. HE WANTS TO GIVE ME THE CROWN! IF HE WERE AS BAD AS YOU SAY HE IS . . .

DON'T TRUST HIM, ELYON . . .

103

DON'T TRUST ANYBODY . . . JUST LISTEN TO YOUR HEART!

ALL RIGHT, PRISONERS!

IT'S DINNERTIME! GET READY!

LOWER YOUR VOICE, JARUS! PRINCESS ELYON IS HERE!

OH! FORGIVE ME, YOUR HIGHNESS!

DON'T WORRY ABOUT IT . . .

I WAS LEAVING ANYWAY.

WE'RE HERE, DAD . . .

STOP THE CAR! THIS IS FINE.

YES, MA'AM!

THANKS FOR THE RIDE, DAD.

NOT A PROBLEM! HAVE FUN!

I'LL TRY! SEE YOU LATER!

PHEW! I REALLY NEED TO GET IN SHAPE . . . BUT RIGHT NOW I HAVE A BIGGER PROBLEM TO SOLVE . . .

. . . HOW TO GET INSIDE WITHOUT A TICKET! I DON'T KNOW HOW WILL DID IT.

BUT I HAVE NO CHOICE. PHOBOS HAS A HOLD OVER ME . . . HE FORCED ME TO TAKE THIS ROLE.

"I HAD NO CHOICE . . ."

GOOD AFTERNOON, DALTAR . . .

YOUR HIGHNESS . . .

I'VE COME DOWN FOR A VISIT! YOU SHOULD FEEL HONORED, GARDENER . . .

I JUST WANTED TO SEE IF THE RUMORS I HAD HEARD FROM THE MURMURERS WERE TRUE!

I DON'T KNOW WHAT YOU ARE TALKING ABOUT, MY LORD.

I WANT YOU TO CREATE ROSES WITH LETHAL THORNS! AN ENORMOUS BARRIER OF FLOWERS BETWEEN MY CASTLE AND MERIDIAN.

ANYONE WHO TOUCHES THE POISONOUS THORNS TURNS INTO ONE OF THE ROSES...

THESE FLOWERS... ARE ACTUALLY THE PEOPLE OF MERIDIAN! THOUSANDS AND THOUSANDS OF DESPERATE SOULS WHO HAVE TRIED TO GET INSIDE THE CASTLE TO ASK PHOBOS FOR MERCY...

SO THESE ROSES... ARE ALIVE?

YES... AND IT IS MY JOB TO TAKE CARE OF THEM! SOMEWHERE INSIDE THESE THICK BUSHES IS MY FAMILY!

BUT I DON'T KNOW WHERE! SO MUCH TIME HAS PASSED SINCE PHOBOS TRANSFORMED THEM... AND SO MANY NEW ROSES HAVE BLOOMED.

COME ON, DALTAR...

BUT THINGS ARE GOING TO CHANGE SOON. I HEARD A RUMOR THAT SOMEONE IS HELPING PEOPLE TO ESCAPE FROM MERIDIAN.

IT'S LORD CEDRIC!

IT'S A TRAP!

WHAT!

HOW VERY CLEVER OF YOU, VATHEK! WE WERE A GOOD TEAM ONCE . . .

GET OUT OF HERE! GO HOME!

QUICK! QUICK!

AHHHHH! EEEEK!

. . . BUT ALL GOOD THINGS MUST COME TO AN END!

AAARGH!

VATHEK!

GOOD-BYE, OLD FRIEND!

GASP!

SORRY FOR THE INTERRUPTION. DID I COME AT A BAD TIME?

WILL! WH—WHE DID YOU C FROM?

HUH?